This book belongs to

....

First published in 2013 by Miles Kelly Publishing Ltd
Harding's Barn, Bardfield End Green, Thaxted, Essex, CM6 3PX, UK

2 4 6 8 10 9 7 5 3 1

Publishing Director Belinda Gallagher
Creative Director Jo Cowan
Editorial Director Rosie McGuire
Senior Designer Joe Jones
Production Manager Elizabeth Collins
Reprographics Stephan Davis, Jennifer Hunt, Thom Allaway

ISBN 978-1-78209-293-3

Printed in China

British Library Cataloguing-in-Publication Data
A catalogue record for this book is available from the British Library

ACKNOWLEDGEMENTS

The publishers would like to thank the following artists
who have contributed to this book:
Cover (main): Karen Sapp at The Bright Agency
Decorative banners (cover and throughout): asmjp from Shutterstock.com
Insides: Cecilia Johansson

Made with paper from a sustainable forest

www.mileskelly.net   info@mileskelly.net

www.factsforprojects.com

The Princess and the Pea

Miles
Kelly

Once upon a time there was a handsome prince. And although he lived in a beautiful palace and had everything he could wish for,

The Princess and the Pea

he was very fed up.
The problem was that
everyone in the court, from

his father, the king, right down to the smallest page, seemed to think it was high time that he got married. The prince would have been very happy to get married, but he did insist that his bride be a real, true, and proper princess.

He held parties and dances all over his kingdom, where he met plenty of perfectly pleasant girls who said they were princesses. But none, it seemed to him, were really true and proper princesses.

Story time

The Princess and the Pea

His search took him to faraway lands, where the royal families presented a host of suitable young ladies. But nowhere could he find a princess who lived up to his high standards. Either their manners were not quite exquisite enough, or their feet were much too big. So he returned to his palace, where he sat reading dusty history books and getting very glum.

One wintery night, there was the most terrible storm. Rain was lashing down,

thunder crashed and
lightning lit up the sky
around the palace. The wind
kept blowing out the candles,
and everyone huddled close
to the fire. Suddenly there
was a great peal from the
huge front doorbell.

And there, absolutely dripping wet, stood a princess. Well, she said she was a princess, but never had anyone looked less like a princess than she did.

Her hair was plastered to her head, her dress was

The Princess and the Pea

wringing wet and her silk
shoes were covered in mud.
She was quite alone, without

even the smallest maid, and just where had she come from? But she kept insisting that she was a princess.

The queen thought this very unlikely, but she couldn't just leave the poor thing shivering on the doorstep, so

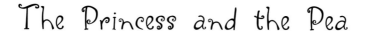

The Princess and the Pea

she invited her in and told
her to take a seat by the fire.
The poor girl sat sipping a
mug of warm milk sweetened
with honey and trying not to
ruin the carpet. As she grew
warmer the prince noticed
how pink her cheeks were, and

how pretty her laugh.

The queen noticed the attention her son was paying this mystery girl, and she decided to test whether or not she really was a princess.

She went to supervise the making of the girl's bed – in

the second-best spare
bedroom, for she didn't think
it was necessary to put their
late-night visitor in the best
spare bedroom (after all she
might turn out to be only an
ordinary duchess).

First the queen told the six

Story time

maids to take all of the bedclothes and the mattress off the bed. Then she placed one single pea right on the middle of the bedstead. Next the maids piled twenty mattresses on top of the pea, and dozens of silk sheets and feather quilts and warm blankets on top of all the mattresses. Then the girl was shown to her room and left for the night.

In the morning, the queen swept into the bedroom in her dressing gown and asked

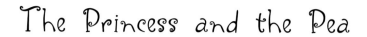

the girl how she had slept.

"I didn't sleep a wink all night," said the girl. "There was a great, hard lump in the middle of the bed. It was quite dreadful. I am sure I am black and blue all over!"

The queen was delighted,

for this meant that the girl really was a princess, for only a true princess could be as sensitive as that.

The prince was overjoyed. He proposed to the princess at once, and they lived very happily ever after.

The Princess and the Pea

The pea was placed in the royal museum, where it probably still is today.

The End